SWISH

The Science Behind Basketball's Most Dynamic Plays

by Allan Morey

CAPSTONE PRESS
a capstone imprint

Published by Capstone Press, an imprint of Capstone
1710 Roe Crest Drive, North Mankato, Minnesota 56003
capstonepub.com

Copyright © 2025 by Capstone. All rights reserved. No part of this publication may be reproduced in whole or in part, or stored in a retrieval system, or transmitted in any form or by any means, electronic, mechanical, photocopying, recording, or otherwise, without written permission of the publisher.

SPORTS ILLUSTRATED KIDS is a trademark of ABG-SI LLC.
Used with permission.

Library of Congress Cataloging-in-Publication Data is available on the Library of Congress website.
ISBN: 9781669091905 (hardcover)
ISBN: 9781669092070 (paperback)
ISBN: 9781669091943 (ebook PDF)

Summary: Discover the science behind legendary basketball plays, including Dr. J's iconic slam dunk, Kobe's epic alley-oop to Shaq, LeBron's massive block against Iguodala, and Jordan's buzzer-beater.

Editorial Credits
Editor: Christianne Jones; Designer: Jaime Willems; Media Researcher: Svetlana Zhurkin; Production Specialist: Whitney Schaefer

Image Credits
Associated Press: Eric Risberg, cover (right); Capstone: Jaime Willems, 26, 27; Getty Images: © 1964 NBAE/Dick Raphael, 19, © 2000 NBAE/Andrew D. Bernstein, 16, 29, © 2016 NBAE/Nathaniel S. Butler, 22, © 2016 NBAE/Noah Graham, 20, Bettmann, 25, Focus on Sport, 7, GeorgiosArt, 9 (Newton), Mark Blinch, 5, Nick Laham, cover (left), Thearon W. Henderson, 1, 23, Tom Hauck, 14, 15; Newscom: Icon SMI/John McDonough, 12, TNS/Raleigh News & Observer, 13, Zumapress/Michael Goulding, 17; Shutterstock: Deviney Designs (powder), cover and throughout, lumyai l sweet, 9 (referee), Marina Sun (math background), cover and throughout, Master1305, 8, MoreVector, 10–11, Virtis (basketball), back cover and throughout; Sports Illustrated: Manny Millan, 28

Any additional websites and resources referenced in this book are not maintained, authorized, or sponsored by Capstone. All product and company names are trademarks™ or registered® trademarks of their respective holders.

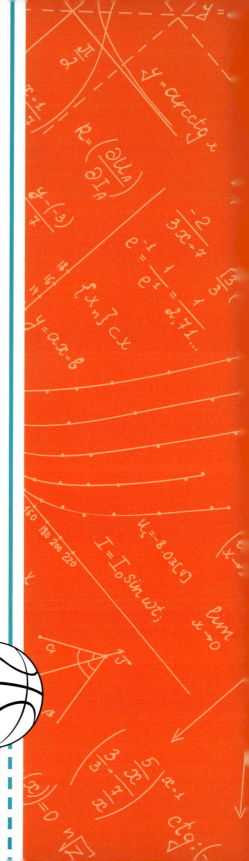

TABLE OF CONTENTS

Science and Basketball 4

Chapter One
Slam Dunk 6

Chapter Two
Alley-oop 13

Chapter Three
The Block 18

Chapter Four
The Shot 24

Glossary 30
Read More 31
Internet Sites 31
Index 32
About the Author 32

Words in **BOLD** are in the glossary.

SCIENCE AND BASKETBALL

From tip-off to final buzzer, basketball is a fast-paced game. Players race up and down the court as they dribble, pass, defend, and shoot. A standard NBA game lasts just 48 minutes. In that time, teams often score more than 100 points. That means each team hits more than a basket per minute. Swish!

To achieve their high-scoring feats, basketball players need to be amazing athletes. They also need science. They need **friction**, **momentum**, and **energy**. They need Newton's three laws of motion.

Let's explore how science affected some of the most memorable plays in NBA history.

DEFINITIONS

energy: force that causes things to move

momentum: the force or speed created by movement

friction: a special kind of force that slows down or stops motion

CHAPTER ONE

SLAM DUNK

One of the most dynamic basketball plays is the slam dunk. Players seem to defy **gravity** as they leap in the air and slam the ball into the basket. Dunking grew in popularity during the 1970s thanks to stars like Julius Erving. Better known as Dr. J, he played for the Philadelphia 76ers.

GRANDFATHERS OF THE DUNK

Joe Fortenberry is credited with the first slam dunk. He was a member of the 1936 U.S. Olympic basketball team. Fortenberry made the dunk during the games in Berlin, Germany. Bob Kurland played college basketball for Oklahoma A&M. In 1944, he made the first slam dunk in college basketball.

On January 5, 1983, Dr. J threw down one of the most iconic dunks in NBA history. The 76ers were in a hard-fought battle against the Los Angeles Lakers. The game went into overtime. Dr. J picked up a tipped pass. He dribbled toward the hoop.

Dr. J used momentum and energy to drive toward the hoop.

DEFINITIONS

gravity: a force that pulls objects toward the ground

potential energy: stored energy

kinetic energy: the energy of motion

force: an action that changes or maintains the motion of a body or object

DEFINITIONS

Dribbling may look simple, but it is full of science. Dribbling applies **force** to a basketball. Like any object, a basketball has **potential energy**. Dropping the ball and letting gravity pull it down turns that potential energy into **kinetic energy**.

When the basketball hits the court, Newton's third law of motion takes over. The ball pushes against the floor. The floor pushes back. The ball bounces up.

FORCE

KINETIC ENERGY

POTENTIAL ENERGY

POTENTIAL ENERGY

KINETIC ENERGY

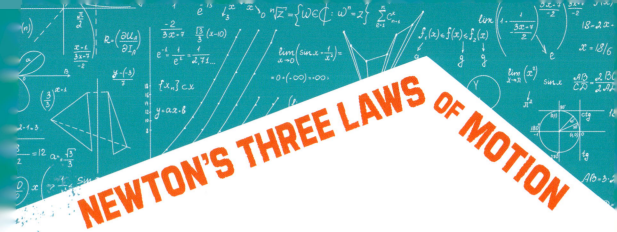

NEWTON'S THREE LAWS OF MOTION

Scientist Isaac Newton developed three rules about motion. These are known as Newton's laws of motion, and they play a huge role in every game.

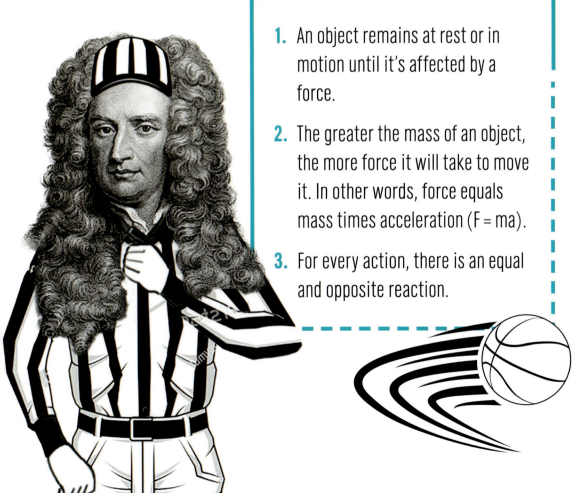

1. An object remains at rest or in motion until it's affected by a force.

2. The greater the mass of an object, the more force it will take to move it. In other words, force equals mass times acceleration (F = ma).

3. For every action, there is an equal and opposite reaction.

Back in the action, Laker Michael Cooper stood between Dr. J and the basket. Cooper was one of the best defenders in the league. He immediately moved to block Dr. J's path. But Dr. J quickly dribbled past him.

Dr. J cradled the ball between the palm of his right hand and his wrist. He swung his arm forward. Then he planted his left foot. What happened next was a matter of energy and power.

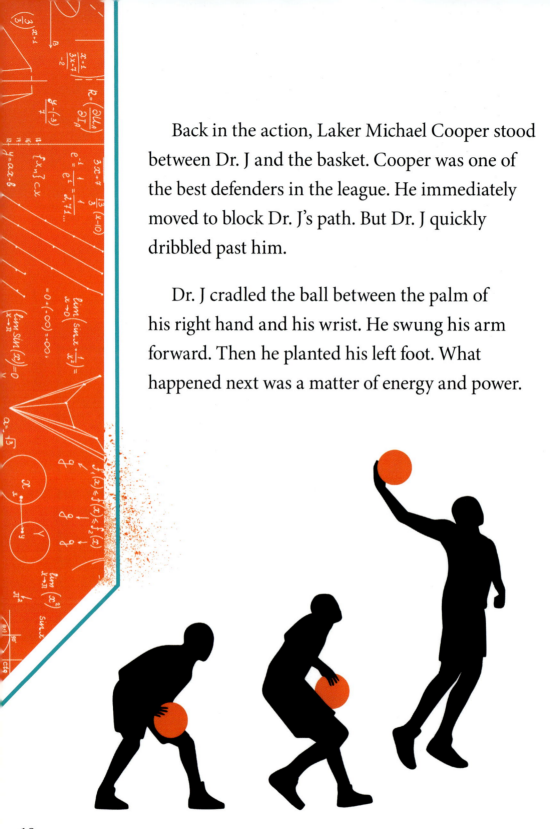

All of Dr. J's kinetic energy from running down the court **transferred** to his left leg. His leg bent, like a spring being pushed down. When he jumped, he straightened his left leg and released that stored energy. This action gave him power to spring toward the hoop.

transfer: to move from one object to another

The speed from Dr. J's windmill arm movement added more force to the dunk.

As Dr. J leaped into the air, he stretched his arm back in a circle. It looked like a windmill turning. He continued to hold the ball, applying force to it with the movement of his arm. The greater the **applied force**, the faster the basketball swung around. WHAM! Dr. J's amazing dunk helped the Sixers beat the Lakers 122–120.

applied force: force used to move an object, such as passing a basketball

CHAPTER TWO

ALLEY-OOP

One of the most jaw-dropping basketball plays is the alley-oop. A player throws a perfect pass to a teammate as the teammate leaps toward the basket. Perhaps the most spectacular alley-oop occurred on June 4, 2000, during Game 7 of the Western Conference Finals.

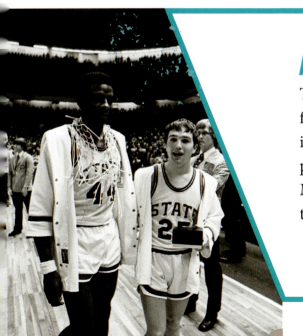

ALLEY-OOP INVENTORS

The first sports alley-oop was actually a football play for the San Francisco 49ers in 1957. North Carolina State University players David Thompson (left) and Monte Towe are credited with bringing the alley-oop to basketball in the 1970s.

Energy flowed through Kobe's body as he pushed the ball up court.

The Portland Trailblazers were looking to upset the Los Angeles Lakers. At the start of the fourth quarter, the Trailblazers were up 71–58. But the Lakers made one of the greatest comebacks in NBA playoff history. With 47 seconds left in the game, the Lakers were up 83–79.

Kobe Bryant had the ball just outside the three-point line. He dribbled around a defender. As Kobe approached the free throw line, two more defenders stood between him and the basket.

In a split-second, he had to decide what to do. He saw Shaquille O'Neal near the basket. But Kobe could not throw the ball directly to him. Defenders were in the way.

Kobe looked over a defender for an open teammate.

Kobe tossed the ball over a defender's hand. Shaq took a step toward the basket and planted his feet. He bent his legs, which stored energy. As Kobe's pass flew over the defender's hand, Shaq turned that potential energy into kinetic energy by leaping to catch the ball.

Shaq used kinetic energy and massive force to complete the play.

Force equals the **mass** of an object and its **acceleration**. In this case, Shaq was the object. Shaq was a big guy, weighing 325 pounds (147 kilograms). When gravity started to pull him back down, he had a huge amount of force to slam the ball through the rim. The Lakers won the game 89–84 and went on to win the 2000 NBA Finals.

DEFINITIONS

acceleration: the change in an object's speed

mass: the amount of matter in an object

CHAPTER THREE

THE BLOCK

Offense is an exciting part of basketball. But defense is just as important. A stolen pass or blocked shot can change a game's outcome. And that is exactly what happened in 2016 during Game 7 of the NBA Finals.

The Cleveland Cavaliers faced the Golden State Warriors. With slightly more than four minutes left, the game was tied at 89–89. Both teams were struggling to break the tie.

THE ART OF THE BLOCK

Bill Russell (above, number 6) played for the Boston Celtics from 1956 to 1969. He was in the league before blocks were an official stat, but he perfected it. Instead of wildly swatting at a shot, he tried to tap the blocked shot to a teammate. It's estimated that he may have averaged six to eight blocks per game.

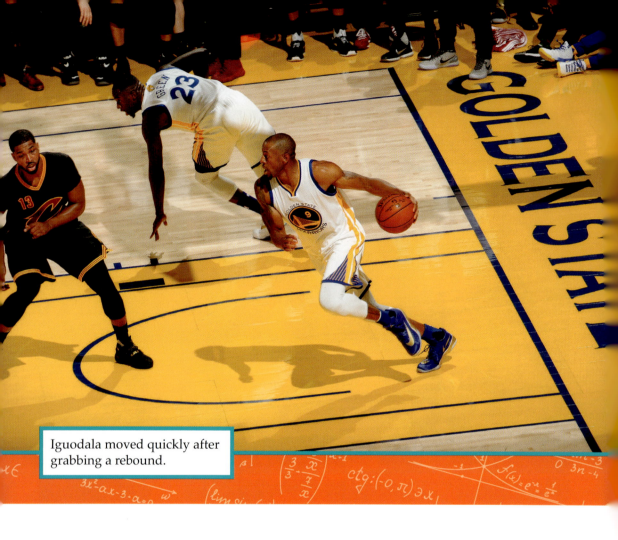

Iguodala moved quickly after grabbing a rebound.

After the Cavs missed a shot, Newton's third law of motion came into play. When one object applies force on another object, the second object adds an equal and opposite force on the first object. The basketball hit the backboard. It then bounced into the hands of Warriors player Andre Iguodala.

With less than two minutes left, Iguodala flew down the court. He turned potential energy into kinetic energy with every dribble. Only J. R. Smith of the Cavs stood in his way. Iguodala applied force to the ball to pass it to teammate Steph Curry.

Smith moved to guard Curry, who passed the ball back to Iguodala. Now Iguodala had a clear path to the basket. He went for a layup. With the basket, Iguodala would have given the Warriors the lead.

But LeBron James of the Cavaliers had other plans. He barreled down the court after Iguodala. He built speed using the friction of his shoes on the floor and the power of his legs. This was Newton's second law of motion. The more force he applied with his legs pushing off the floor, the faster he ran. That meant he was increasing his kinetic energy.

LeBron (right) used kinetic energy to push his body into the air.

As Iguodala went for the layup, LeBron also sprung into the air. He was using his built-up kinetic energy. His momentum carried him toward the basket. As the ball went up to bounce off the backboard, LeBron slapped it away. He had blocked the shot!

FACT

Blocks were not an official NBA stat until the 1973–74 season.

LeBron's block not only preserved the tie, but the big play sparked his team. The Cavs won 93–89. LeBron had three blocks as he helped his team become the NBA champions.

LeBron timed his jump perfectly to block Iguodala's shot.

CHAPTER FOUR

THE SHOT

Basketball history includes many dynamic plays. But only one is known as "The Shot." And who made it? Basketball legend Michael Jordan. Of course, he had a little help from science.

It was Game 5 of the first round of the 1989 Eastern Conference playoffs. Jordan's Chicago Bulls were in a close game against the Cleveland Cavaliers. The winner of this game would move on, while the losing team was done for the season.

With just three seconds left, Cavs player Craig Ehlo hit a layup to give his team the lead. But there was still enough time for one more shot. Everyone knew the Bulls would try to get the ball to Jordan.

Ehlo and teammate Larry Nance double-teamed Jordan. But Jordan faked right, tricking Nance. Nance's momentum put Newton's first law of motion into effect. Once moving, Nance couldn't easily stop. This left Jordan open.

With his quick movements, Jordan made it hard for opponents to defend him.

Teammate Brad Sellers inbounded the pass to him. Jordan quickly dribbled around Ehlo. As the clock ticked down to zero, he leaped and took his shot. He was near the free throw line, which is 15 feet from the basket.

While a shot from 15 feet may not seem like much, it's a miracle of science. In a split second, the player has to judge the distance from the basket *and* the width of the target. The farther away a player is from the basket, the narrower the target becomes.

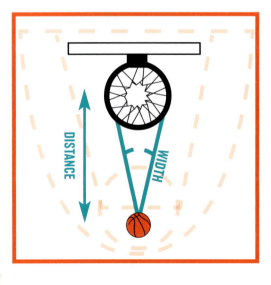
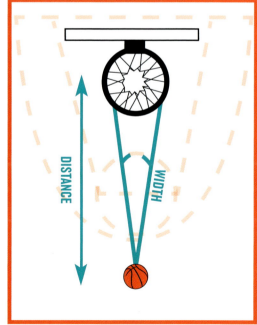

The distance affects the shot's angle. The angle affects the size of the target. From a distance, the circular rim changes to more of an oval target. The greater the angle of the shot, the more room there is available for the ball to go through the hoop. If the angle of the shot is too low, there isn't enough room for the ball to go through the hoop.

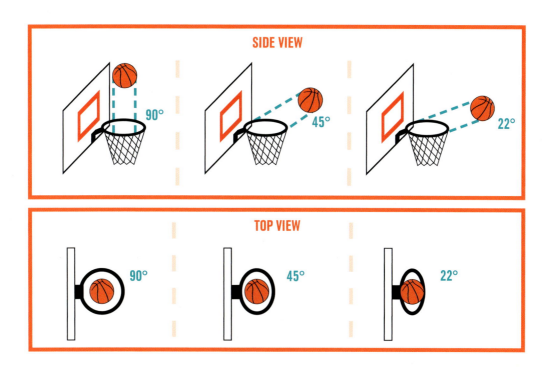

On top of all of that, Jordan was shooting over another player. But Jordan and science were unstoppable. The ball swished into the basket as the buzzer sounded. The Bulls won!

Kobe Bryant seems to defy gravity as he leaps to block a shot.

It's easy to see why basketball captivates fans. The high-flying alley-oops. The massive blocks. The game-winning baskets. It's now easy to see how science is involved in the game too. In fact, science might be the true star.

GLOSSARY

acceleration (ak-sel-uh-REY-shuhn)—the change in an object's speed

applied force (uh-PLAHYD FOHRS)—force used to move an object, such as passing a basketball

energy (EH-nuhr-jee)— force that causes things to move

force (FOHRS)—an action that changes or maintains the motion of a body or object

friction (FRIK-shuhn)—a special kind of force that slows down or stops motion

gravity (GRAH-vuh-tee)—an invisible force that pulls objects toward each other; Earth's gravity pulls objects toward the ground

kinetic energy (ki-NET-ik EH-nuhr-jee)—the energy of motion

mass (MAS)—the amount of matter in an object

momentum (moh-MEN-tuhm)—the force or speed created by movement

potential energy (puh-TEN-shuhl EH-nuhr-jee)—stored energy

READ MORE

Enzo, George. *Physical Science in Basketball*. New York. Crabtree Publishing, 2020.

Helget, N. *Full STEAM Basketball*. North Mankato, MN: Capstone, 2019.

Smith, Elliott. *Basketball's Best Traditions and Weirdest Superstitions*. North Mankato, MN: Capstone, 2023.

INTERNET SITES

Ducksters: Physics for Kids
ducksters.com/science/physics

KiwiCo: Basketball Science
kiwico.com/blog/the-science-behind/basketball-science

National Inventors Hall of Fame: Explore the Science of Basketball
invent.org/blog/trends-stem/science-of-basketball

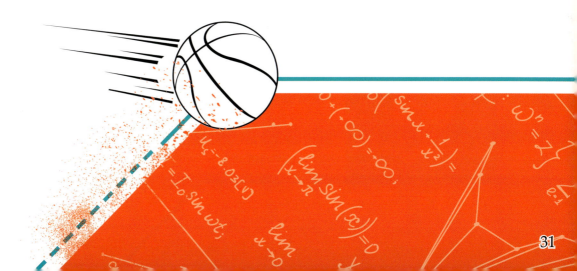

INDEX

acceleration, 9, 17
alley-oop, 13, 29
angles, 27

blocks, 18–19, 22–23, 29
Bryant, Kobe, 14–16

Curry, Steph, 21

energy, 4, 7–8, 10–11, 14, 16, 21–22
Erving, Julius (Dr. J), 6–7, 10–12

force, 4, 7–9, 12, 16–17, 20–21, 30
Fortenberry, Joe, 6
friction, 4, 21

gravity, 6–8, 17, 29

Iguodala, Andre, 20–23

James, LeBron, 21–23
Jordan, Michael, 24–26, 28

layup, 21–22, 25

mass, 9, 17
momentum, 4, 7, 22, 25

Newton's Laws of Motion, 8–9, 20–21, 25

O'Neal, Shaquille (Shaq), 15–17

slam dunk, 6–7, 12, 17
speed, 4, 12, 17, 21

ABOUT THE AUTHOR

Some of Allan Morey's favorite childhood memories are from the time he spent on a farm in Wisconsin. Every day he saw cows, chickens, and sheep. He even had a pet pig named Pete. He developed a great appreciation of animals, big and small. Allan currently lives in St. Paul, Minnesota, with his family and dogs, Stitch and Enzo, who keep him company while he writes children's books.